Library and Information Service

Library materials must be returned on or before the
last due date or fines will be charged at the current
rate. Items can be renewed by telephone, email or by
visting the website, letter or personal call unless
required by another borrower. For hours of opening
and charges see notices displayed in libraries.
Tel: 03333 704700
Email: libraries@lewisham.gov.uk
www.lewisham.gov.uk/libraries

1 J   12|19

PIRATES

Steve Barlow and Steve Skidmore

Illustrated

D1356308

Franklin Watts
First published in Great Britain in 2019 by The Watts Publishing Group

Credits
Design Manager: Peter Scoulding
Cover Designer: Cathryn Gilbert
Illustrations: Santy Gutiérrez
HB ISBN 978 1 4451 5988 1
PB ISBN 978 1 4451 5989 8
Library ebook ISBN 978 1 4451 5990 4

Printed in China.

MIX
Paper from
responsible sources
FSC® C104740
FSC
www.fsc.org

Franklin Watts
An imprint of
Hachette Children's Group
Part of The Watts Publishing Group
Carmelite House
50 Victoria Embankment
London EC4Y 0DZ

An Hachette UK Company
www.hachette.co.uk

www.franklinwatts.co.uk

THE BADDIES

Lord and Lady Evil

Dr Y

They want to rule the galaxy.

THE GOODIES

Boo Hoo   Jet   Tip

They want to stop them.

Deep space.

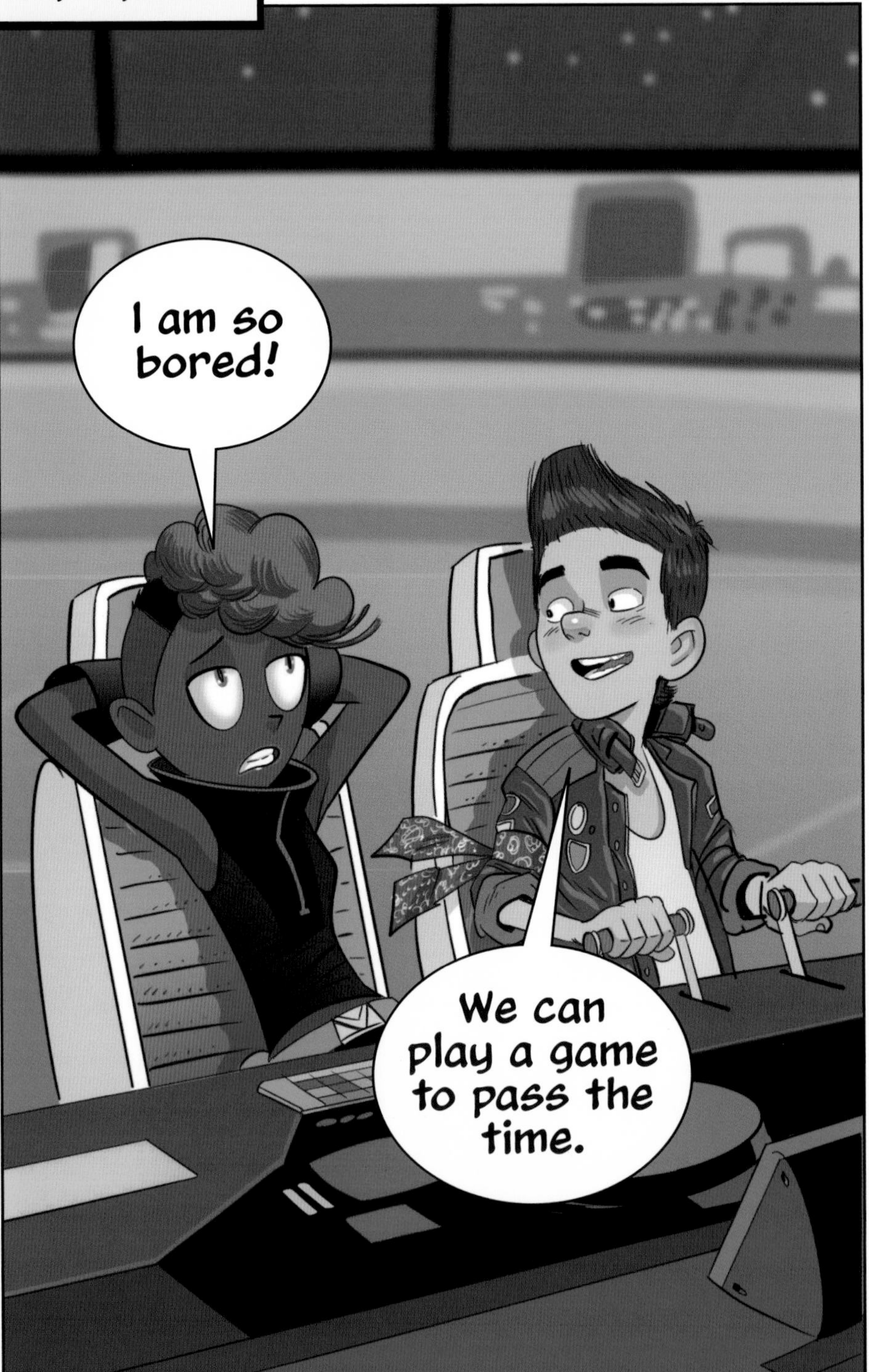

Master Boss told them about the
cargo ship. "We think it is full of gold.
We want you to steal it!"

"Great!" said Jet.

"We are going to be Space Pirates!"
said Tip. "Oo-ar!"

Jet shook her head. "Not funny."

The Goodies set off.

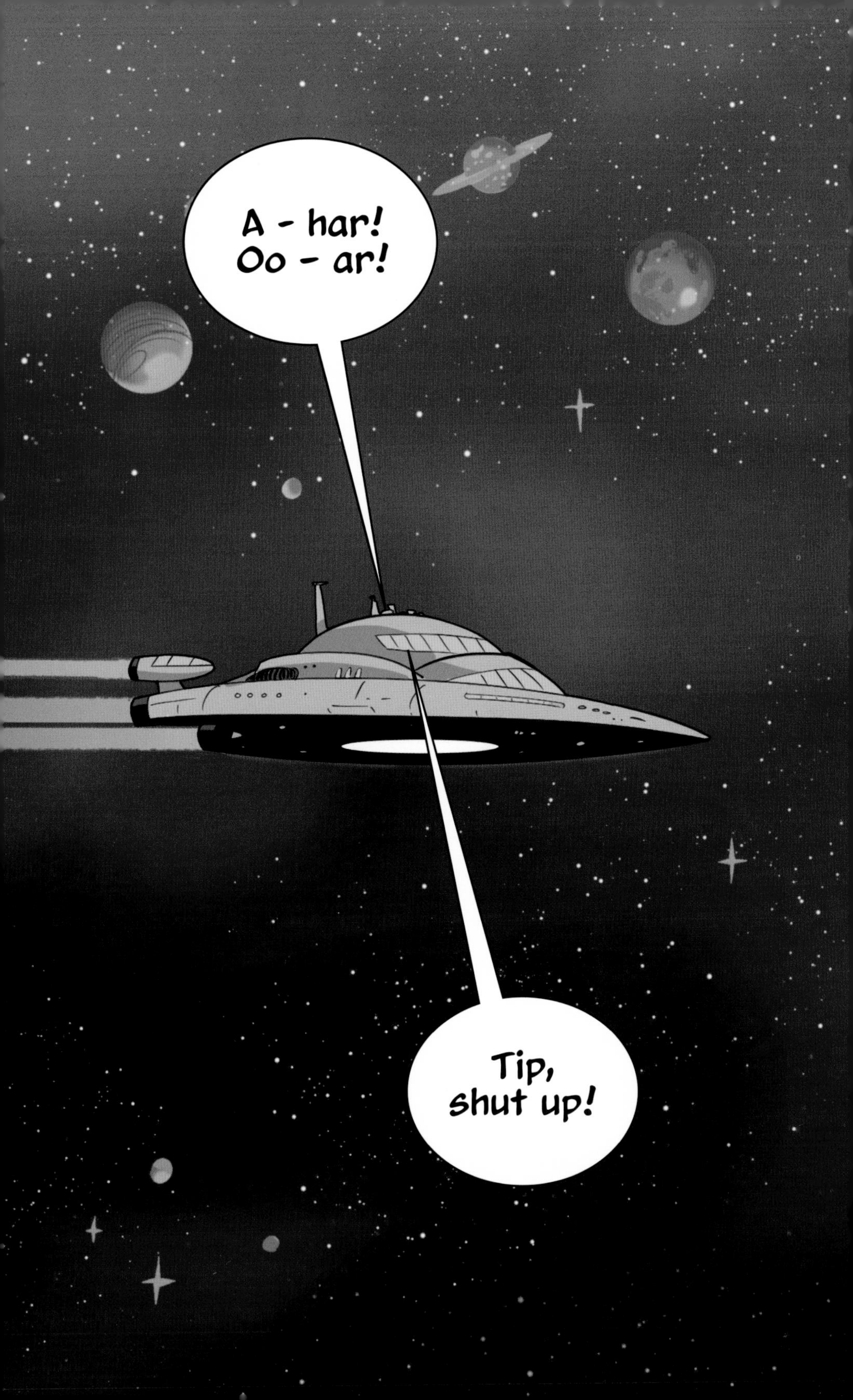
A - har! Oo - ar!
Tip, shut up!

Gold, here we come!

Tip and Jet set the explosive charges.

They went back to Shawn the Ship.

Minutes later, the Baddies arrived.

They headed onto the cargo ship.

27